This book belongs to:
And of course, to me,
Alien Eraser!

ALIEN ERASER
IN
WINDS
OF CHANGE
SO FAR, SO GOOD. THE BOY HAS WRITTEN ABOUT ME.
MAX DISASTER #1
MAX DISASTER #2
BUT I NEED MORE, ALWAYS MORE. IF I AM NOT GROWING AND CHANGING . . .
THEN THE WHOLE WORLD MEANS NOTHING.
I'M JUST A TINY SPECK AMONG BILLIONS OF SPECKS.
NO!
ALIEN ERASER REFUSES AN EXISTENCE OF MEDIOCRITY. EVERYTHING HE DOES MUST BE MAGNIFICENT.
EVEN MY PERSONAL HYGIENE IS SUPERB.

But more than that, Alien Eraser must make a difference. He must use his superior powers to change the world.
Actually, I already HAVE—I just need to let the boy know so he'll write about it.
Strange to think that humans consider themselves to be so highly evolved. I mean, look at him!
GNARRR
GNARRRR
I guess compared to his ancestors millions of years ago, there's SOME improvement—thanks to me!
Evolution of stick figures
Does Alien Eraser really deserve the credit for humanity's superior evolutionary level, or is he just blowing hot air? To find out, TURN THE PAGE!

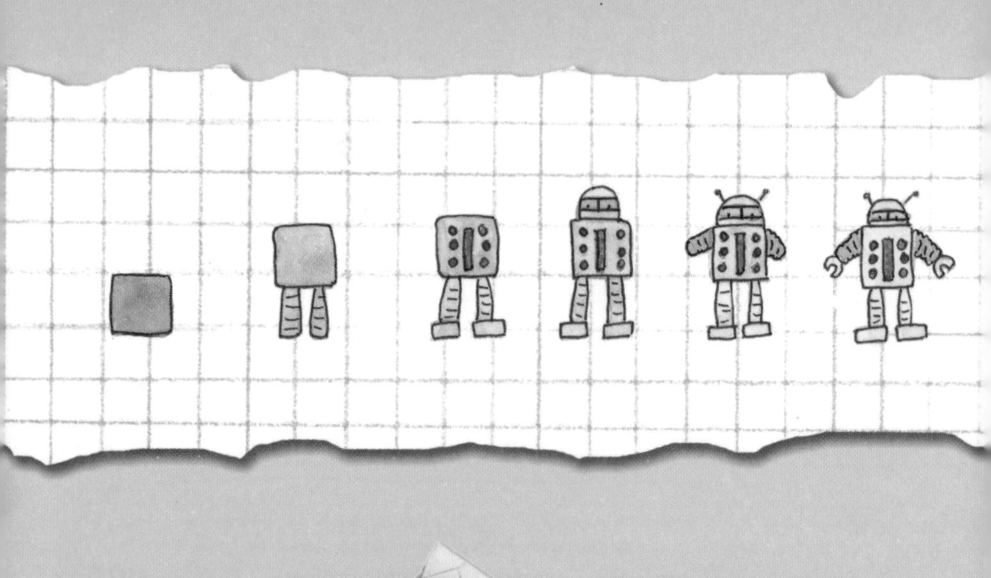

THIS IS MY BOOK FOR WRITING SCIENTIFIC STUFF IN. I FOUND IT ONE MORNING UNDER MY PILLOW. I THINK IT WAS A PRESENT FROM MY MOM. SHE AND MY DAD ARE BOTH SCIENTISTS. I'M GOING TO BE ONE, TOO.

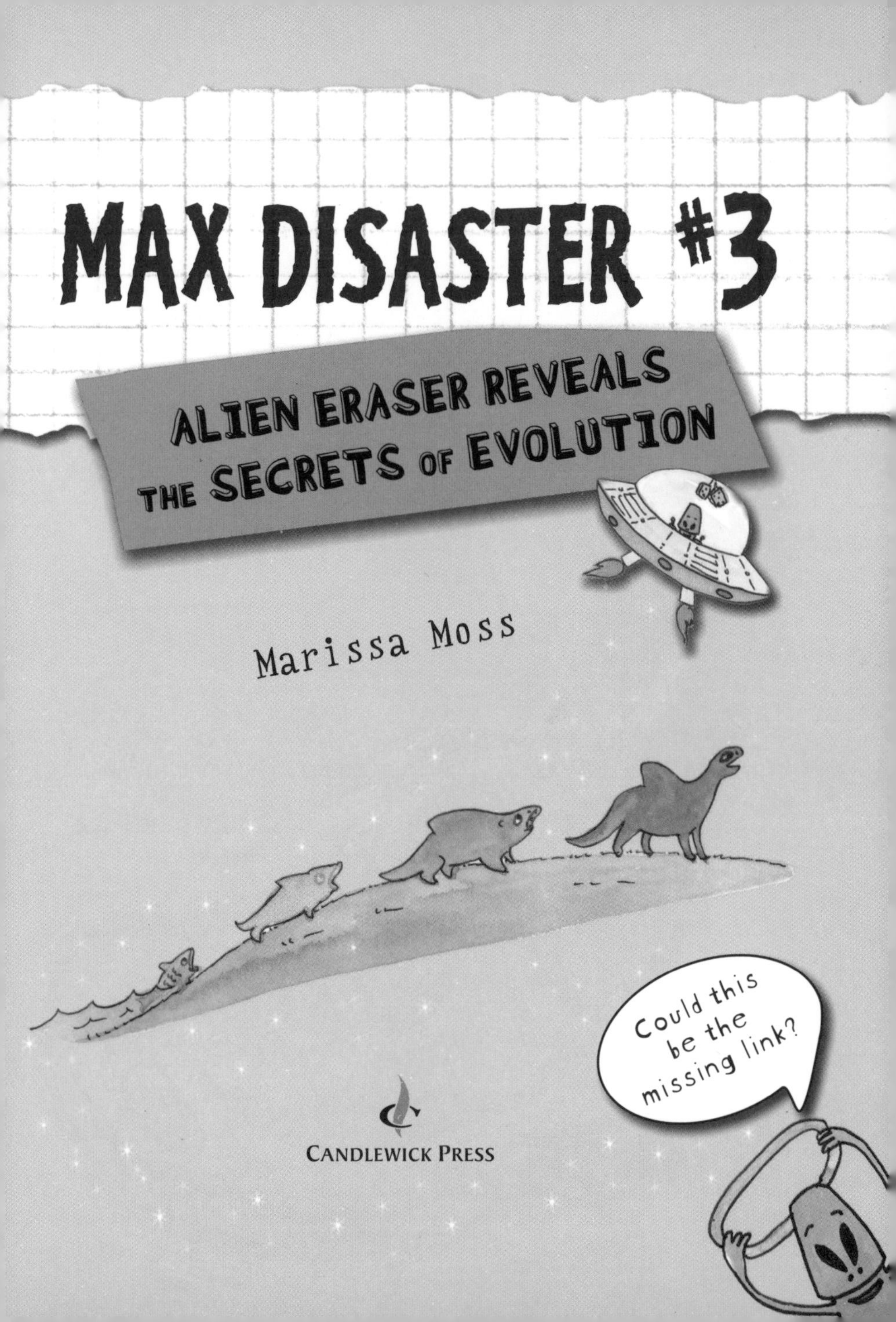
MAX DISASTER #3
ALIEN ERASER REVEALS THE SECRETS OF EVOLUTION
Marissa Moss
Could this be the missing link?
CANDLEWICK PRESS

I thought I knew exactly what I was going to be when I grew up—a scientist. Not just because Mom and Dad are scientists, but because I'm good at science, too.

I love to see what happens when I mix stuff together. So far I haven't blown up anything or started any fires.

But have you made the Elixir of Life?

Well, I THOUGHT I was good at science. My last experiment was a big dud. I found an ancient Egyptian recipe for a love potion and decided to try it on Mom and Dad. Even though Mom and Dad are separated, if the potion worked and they fell in love all over again, it would be as if none of the past year had happened. Dad would move back in, and we'd be a regular family again.

HAVING DRUNK THIS STRANGE CONCOCTION, I FEEL ODD, LIKE I'M IN LOVE WITH YOU!

ME, TOO. LET US STAY TOGETHER FOREVER . . .

IN THIS LIFE AND THE NEXT!

Only the potion didn't work. Maybe it's only good for ancient Egyptians, not modern Americans. Whatever the reason, not only are Mom and Dad still separated, but last night Mom had a date with a man who WAS NOT DAD. It was the grossest thing I'd seen in a looooong time! And living with Kevin, I see some pretty gross stuff.

KEVIN POPPING PIMPLES—
DOESN'T HE KNOW THAT
POPPED PIMPLES ARE WAAAY
WORSE THAN UNPOPPED ONES?

Max's Top Ten on the Gross-O-Meter Scale

10. Unidentified green particles in food.

Pizza is not supposed to have any green on it!

9. Unidentified particles (of any color) in someone else's mouth.

chomp! chomp!
What are you talking about? chomp! chomp!
My table manners are fine.

8. Unidentified (but definitely stinky) glop stuck to the bottom of your shoe. Eew!

La, la, la, la, la!
Gag! Retch!
Bloorfff!

7. Listening to someone get sick.

6. Searching through the garbage for the homework you threw away by mistake.

Maybe if I wipe off the wet coffee grounds and slimy eggshells, I can still turn it in.

5. An overflowing toilet.

Thar she blows!
BLOOOOP!

4. My teacher, Ms. Blodge, dressed up like Little Bo Peep for Halloween.

My students are like my flock, and I am their good shepherd.

3. Kevin's pimples.

Just wait until you get a little older, brat!

2. Finding Crud at the bottom of your glass AFTER you drank from it.

What's so gross about that?

And the number one grossest thing on my top ten list is . . .

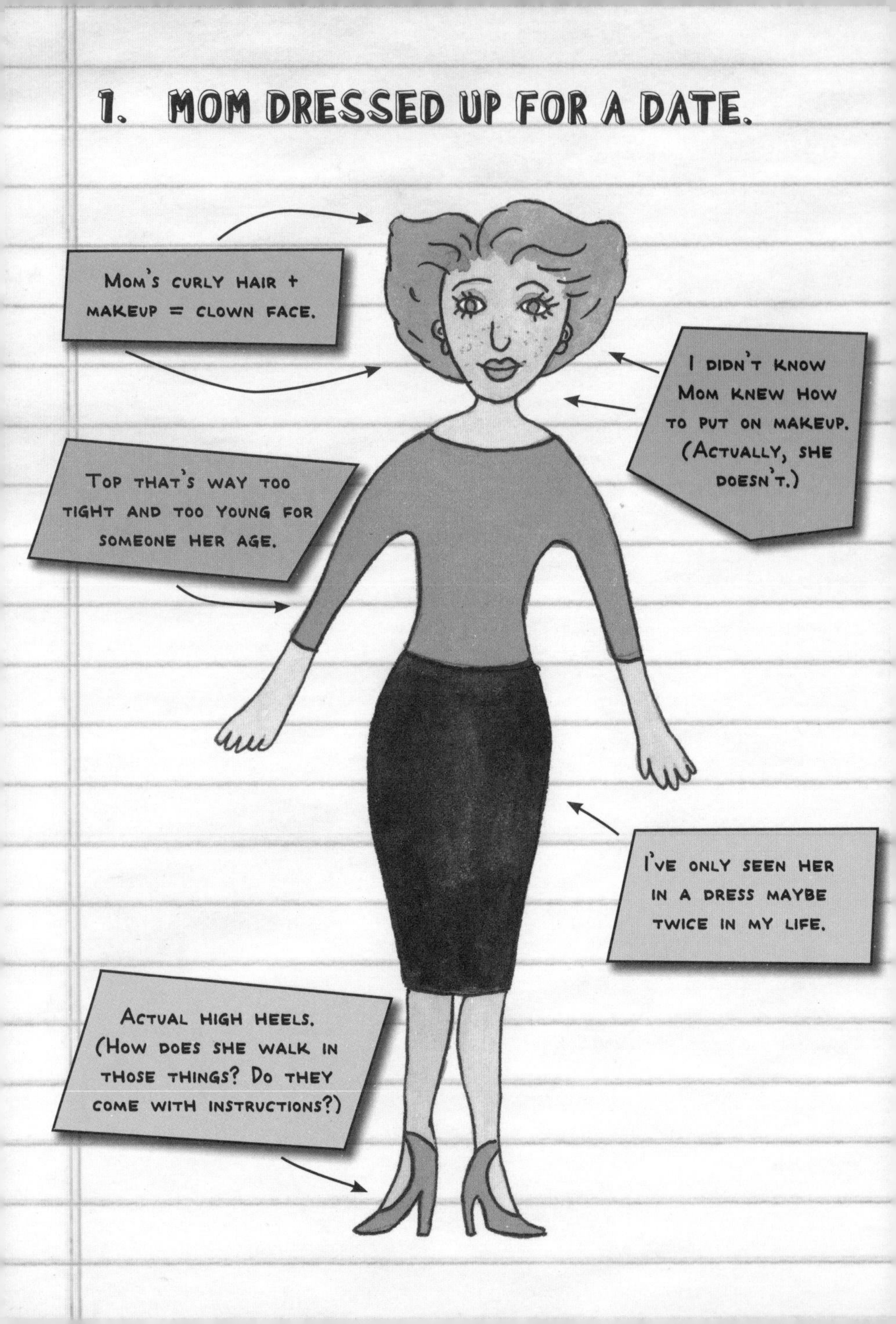
1. MOM DRESSED UP FOR A DATE.
MOM'S CURLY HAIR + MAKEUP = CLOWN FACE.
I DIDN'T KNOW MOM KNEW HOW TO PUT ON MAKEUP. (ACTUALLY, SHE DOESN'T.)
TOP THAT'S WAY TOO TIGHT AND TOO YOUNG FOR SOMEONE HER AGE.
I'VE ONLY SEEN HER IN A DRESS MAYBE TWICE IN MY LIFE.
ACTUAL HIGH HEELS. (HOW DOES SHE WALK IN THOSE THINGS? DO THEY COME WITH INSTRUCTIONS?)

Like I said, it was the most disgusting thing I'd seen in a long time. It was like she'd been abducted by aliens and replaced with a Mombot. Mom wasn't even acting like Mom.

What kind of mom says things like that? An evil alien Mombot, that's who!

Here I thought I was finally getting used to my parents living apart and my having to go back and forth between their places, and now everything changes again.

After she left, of course, we had to wait up worrying about her. When she finally came home (at 11:48 P.M.), Kevin was steamed.

You said you'd be back around eleven. It's close to midnight! Where were you? We've been worried sick. We thought something terrible had happened to you.

But Mom just laughed and said what had happened to her was that she had a wonderful time.

It was so nice to go to a concert. I haven't been to one in such a long time. It's cute of you to worry about me, but I'm a grown-up. I can take care of myself.

I swear this is NOT my mother. My mother would have stayed home, read a boring book, and gone to bed early. She's not supposed to go out and have fun. That's OUR job—we're the kids!

Normally I love making comics. But after last night, I couldn't get into Alien Eraser and his adventures. How can an alien eraser possibly understand what a human boy is going through?

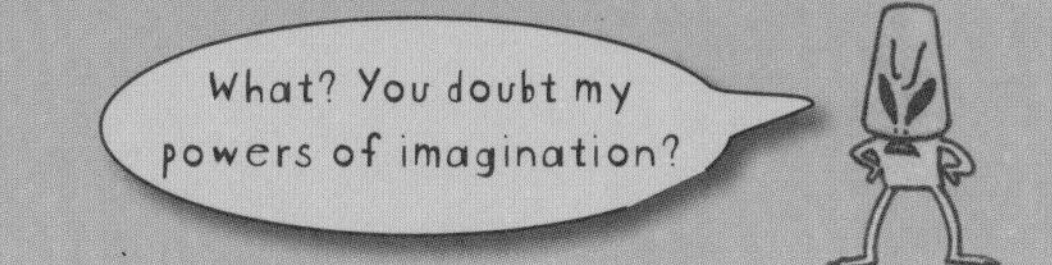

I just let my best friend, Omar, do the drawing.

Alien Eraser
in
The Great Mystery
Alien Eraser has traveled through time and built many great works.
Not bad, if I say so myself.
But his work is far from over. Little does he know he will soon face the greatest challenge of all.
What could it be?
Yes! It is up to Alien Eraser and Alien Eraser alone to solve the mystery of the universe.
Wow!
How cosmic!
Are we alone in the universe? Clearly not, for there is, after all, Alien Eraser.
So the question is, Who else is out there and where are they?
And are they intelligent?
I'm off to explore . . .
the galaxy!
To find out what Alien Eraser discovers, read the next issue of ALIEN ERASER!

After lunch at school, Omar and I were walking to class. Omar's parents have been divorced a long time. His dad is even remarried. I never thought of how weird that must be for him, but now I do. I wanted to ask him about it, but before I could say anything, HE said something to ME.

HEY, MY DAD SAID HE SAW YOUR MOM AT A RESTAURANT LAST NIGHT. DID SHE TELL YOU?
NO, SHE DIDN'T MENTION IT.

What a nightmare! I wanted to ask a zillion questions. Like was my mom smiling and laughing a lot? And what about the guy? Was he fat? bald? Did he tell bad jokes? Were they holding hands? Did they kiss?

GROSS, GROSS, GROSS!

Actually, I didn't want to know—not any of it.

Psst! I can tell you! I see everything!

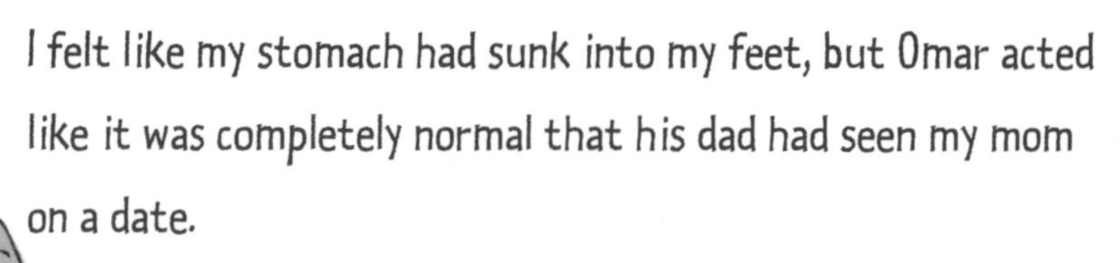

I felt like my stomach had sunk into my feet, but Omar acted like it was completely normal that his dad had seen my mom on a date.

Suddenly I had a horrible headache. Sitting in class with Ms. Blodge only made it worse. Of all the teachers I've had in my life, Ms. Blodge is definitely the worst. Omar calls her "The Blomb." She's already taken away an army of my alien erasers, but I just keep making more.

CONFISCATION!

If she thinks you're daydreaming, then you're really in trouble. Lucky for me, I'm an expert at looking like I'm paying attention when really I'm not.

How to avoid being noticed by Ms. Blodge

Steps:

1. Keep eyes open wide so that you seem alert.
2. Hold pencil at the ready, as if you can't wait to record the pearls of wisdom pouring from your teacher's lips.
3. Lean forward in your chair so you look eager to learn. (Slouching gets you noticed, and getting noticed gets you detention.)
4. Keep your face as blank as possible. (No smiling – that makes you look like you're planning some sneaky trick.)

Results:

Now you're ready to daydream all you want without the risk of being called on.

Except today my daydreams were more like day*mares.* I kept thinking about Mom and her date and that's something I DIDN'T want to imagine.

So I did something I rarely do. I paid attention to Ms. Blodge!

CLASS, TODAY WE'RE STARTING OUR UNIT ON EVOLUTION. EVOLUTION IS HOW A SPECIES CHANGES OVER TIME IN ORDER TO ADAPT TO ITS ENVIRONMENT.

The animals with the best traits to fit their environments survive, then breed to make more animals with the same successful characteristics. The others die out and don't pass on their genes to the species.

That made me think about what traits people have that help our species survive, and what traits don't do us much good. Like little toes and eyebrows. What good are they? Shouldn't they have evolved away by now?

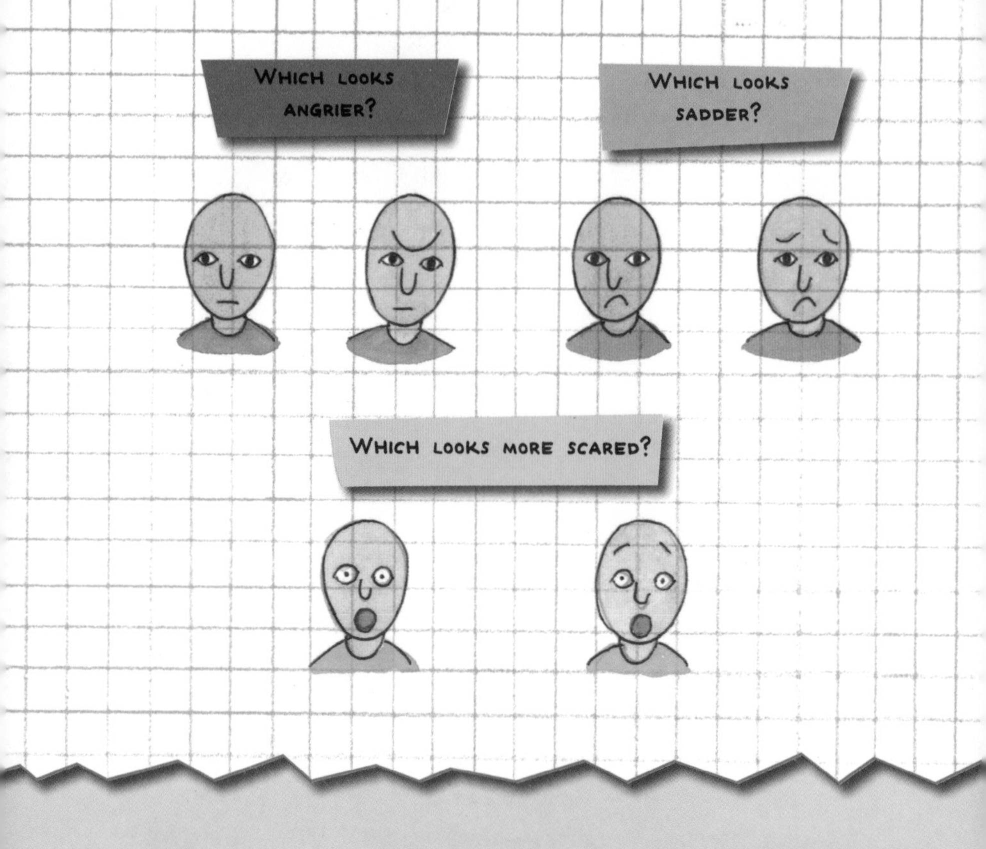

I take it back—we really do need eyebrows. Without them, it's hard to tell what people are feeling, and that's something you need to know—for survival even! Uh-oh, I was so busy thinking about the evolution of eyebrows, I forgot to pay attention to Ms. Blodge. Now I don't know what the homework is for today. You would think I'd have evolved a way to listen to Ms. Blodge and doodle in my logbook at the same time.

While I may not have Alien Eraser's superior brain and skills, I do have Omar for a best friend. He DID write down the homework, so I'm saved! At least from Ms. Blodge.

WOE TO YOU, PUNY EARTHLING!
If you were a superior species like Alien Eraser, all necessary information would be etched into your brain, allowing you to do homework flawlessly and to ace all tests and pop quizzes.

When I got home, Mom was on the phone. I had a feeling she was talking to Mr. X, or whatever her date's name was. It was disgusting. One date and she's acting like a . . . like a . . . I dunno—like a teenager!

What's wrong with this picture?

1. The apple in the bowl has a worm in it.
2. The calendar page is on the wrong month. (Someone seems to have forgotten to turn it. Does she even know what year it is?)
3. Mom is talking on the phone, not greeting her children when they come home from school.
4. The person on the other end of the phone should be a politician or an encyclopedia salesperson, not Mom's boyfriend.
5. Mom is smiling too much and laughing too loud.
6. Mom's toenails are a strange color. (Since when did she start using nail polish?)
7. Mom should not be leaning back in her chair like some kid, but acting her age.
8. Mom should be busy making her son's favorite meal for dinner.
9. There is no ice cream in the freezer for dessert.
10. Mom hasn't cleaned up spill on floor.

I slammed the refrigerator door really loud and made as much noise as I could while I got a snack. Mom finally got the hint, said she had to go, and hung up the phone. About time!

MAX, CAN WE TALK ABOUT THIS?

I didn't say anything. There's nothing to talk about.

You're too old to date. Period. End of sentence.

After a while, Mom gave up and went away, which was fine with me.

But there's always something to talk about!

I guess the evolution homework is seeping into my comics. I finished a new one just before Dad came to pick up Kevin and me for the weekend.

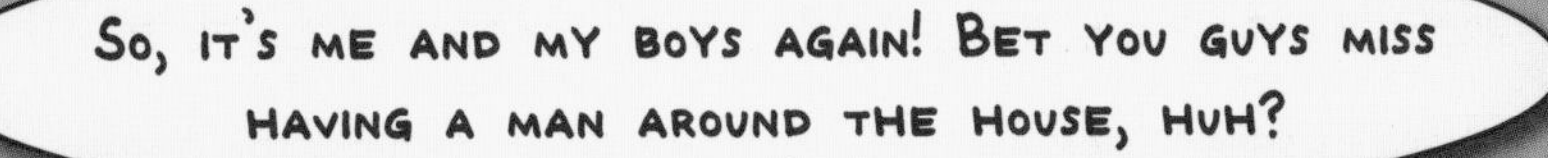

Dad seemed to guess that something was up. When Kevin and I didn't say anything, there was a long silence, as heavy and thick as wet cement.

It was the most uncomfortable weekend at Dad's in a long time. Dad moped, Kevin wouldn't talk (except to tell me to shut up), and there was nothing to do. So I worked on some new inventions. At least that helped me feel scientific again, something I haven't felt much lately.

Invention #2
Body Spring
Defense Against the Buddy-Buddy Type
Hand reaches out to pat boy on back.
What say we shoot some hoops?
What say we don't! Hee, hee!
BOOOIING!
Boy flips switch to activate spring action in specially wired suit.
Boy magically swings out of reach, evading the Buddy-Buddy pat.

Invention #3
Army of Robot Brothers
DADDY!
DADDY!
DADDY!
DEFENSIVE SCARE TACTIC
DADDY!
DADDY!
DADDY!
DADDY!
DADDY!
DADDY!
I THOUGHT YOU SAID YOU ONLY HAD TWO KIDS!
DADDY!
PANICKED DATE EXITS, NEVER TO BE SEEN AGAIN!

That takes care of potential dates for Mom!

Now for Dad, it's even simpler. Women are much easier to scare off than men!

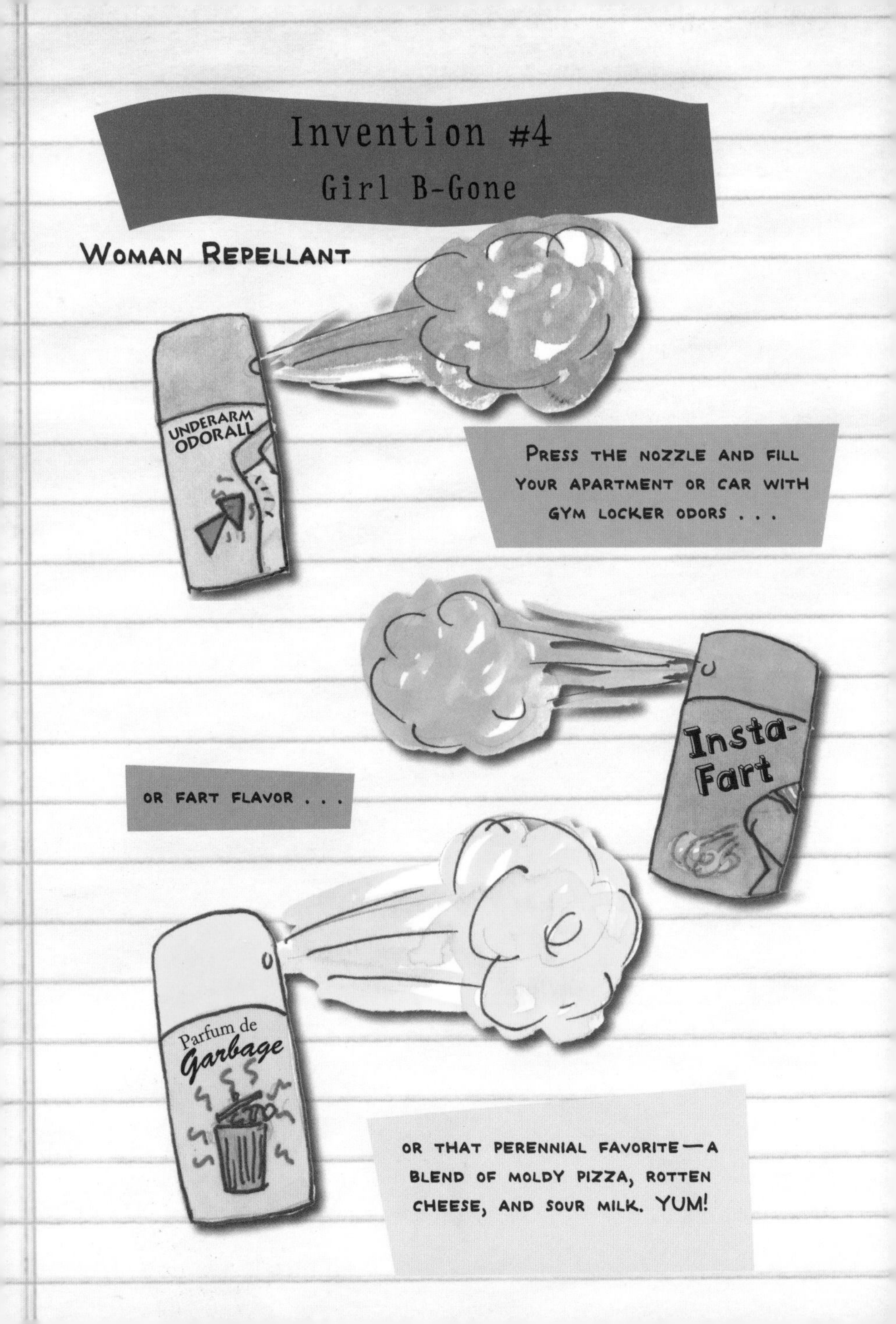
Invention #4
Girl B-Gone
Woman Repellant
UNDERARM ODORALL
Press the nozzle and fill your apartment or car with gym locker odors . . .
Insta-Fart
or fart flavor . . .
Parfum de Garbage
or that perennial favorite—a blend of moldy pizza, rotten cheese, and sour milk. YUM!

Invention #5
Pet Peeves
SURE TO WARD OFF ANY UNWANTED FEMALE GUEST.
DOES THE NICE LADY WANT TO PET THORWALD? HE'S SUCH A SWEET TARANTULA!
UM, NO THANK YOU.
INFLATABLE RATS TARANTULAS, SNAKES, HISSING COCKROACHES, AN OTHER REPULSIVE PETS.
HOW ABOUT CLINT, MY PET BOA CONSTRICTOR? YOU CAN HOLD HIM IF YOU LIKE.
UH, I JUST REMEMBERED THAT THERE'S THIS THING I HAVE TO DO— LEAVE! BYE-BYE!

Invention #6
Slob-in-a-Can
Pop the top and out comes an instant pigsty!
Spaghetti sauce stains
Crushed potato chips
Wadded-up tissues
Banana peels
Stale bread crumbs
Ah, looks and feels like home!
Nail clippings
Dust bunnies
Moldy, half-eaten donut
Guaranteed to turn any place into a seedy, gross pit.

Invention #7
Hunchback of Notre-Dame Kit
WARD OFF POTENTIAL SUITORS WITH YOUR OWN MONSTER.
INSERT FOAM HUMP—THE REST IS UP TO YOU!
UM, YOU DIDN'T MENTION THAT YOUR SON WAS SO SPECIAL.
Those inventions made me feel much better! I showed them to Kevin, and he loved them. His favorite is the Robot Brother Army.
NOT BAD, BRO!
I thought *I* was his favorite.

Our house would be so noisy, our own parents wouldn't be able to stand it, much less a complete stranger.

After not saying anything about Mom all weekend, Dad brought her up Sunday night, like he knew she was what was on our minds.

So, um, I understand your mom is dating again.

Wow! News sure does travel fast in a small town.

Kevin just shrugged. He's an expert at that. But suddenly I had an idea. Maybe Dad was just the person to help.

YOU HAVE TO SAVE US!
Mom's dating some creep! I mean, he's probably an ax murderer or something, and after he does away with Mom, we're next. You have to make her come to her senses. She's acting totally irresponsible and un-momlike.

Okay, maybe I overdid it a little, but it was a drastic situation that called for drastic measures.

NOW MAX, YOUR MOTHER HAS BETTER TASTE THAN THAT. AFTER ALL, SHE MARRIED ME!

YEAH, AND NOW SHE WANTS A DIVORCE. IS THAT GOOD TASTE?

Now me, I have the best taste—absolutley delicious!

It was definitely an untasty dinner that night.

Dad sighed. "We've talked about this before. Sometimes two people can start out loving one another, then they change or grow apart. That doesn't mean they're bad; they're just different from the way they used to be."

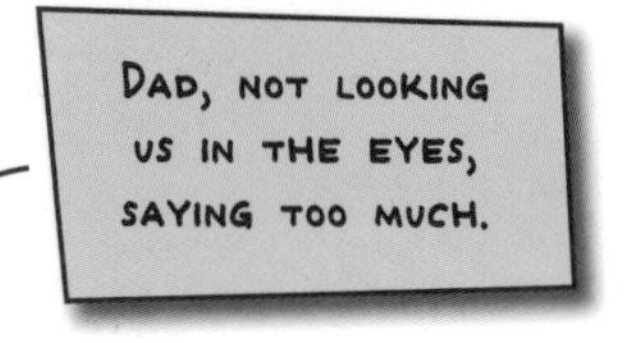

Dad, not looking us in the eyes, saying too much.

Kevin, looking at his plate, saying nothing
Me, following Kevin's example

There was nothing else to say, but I wondered, can people change and still love each other? I mean if you can change one way, why can't you change back? What if a change is NOT an improvement?

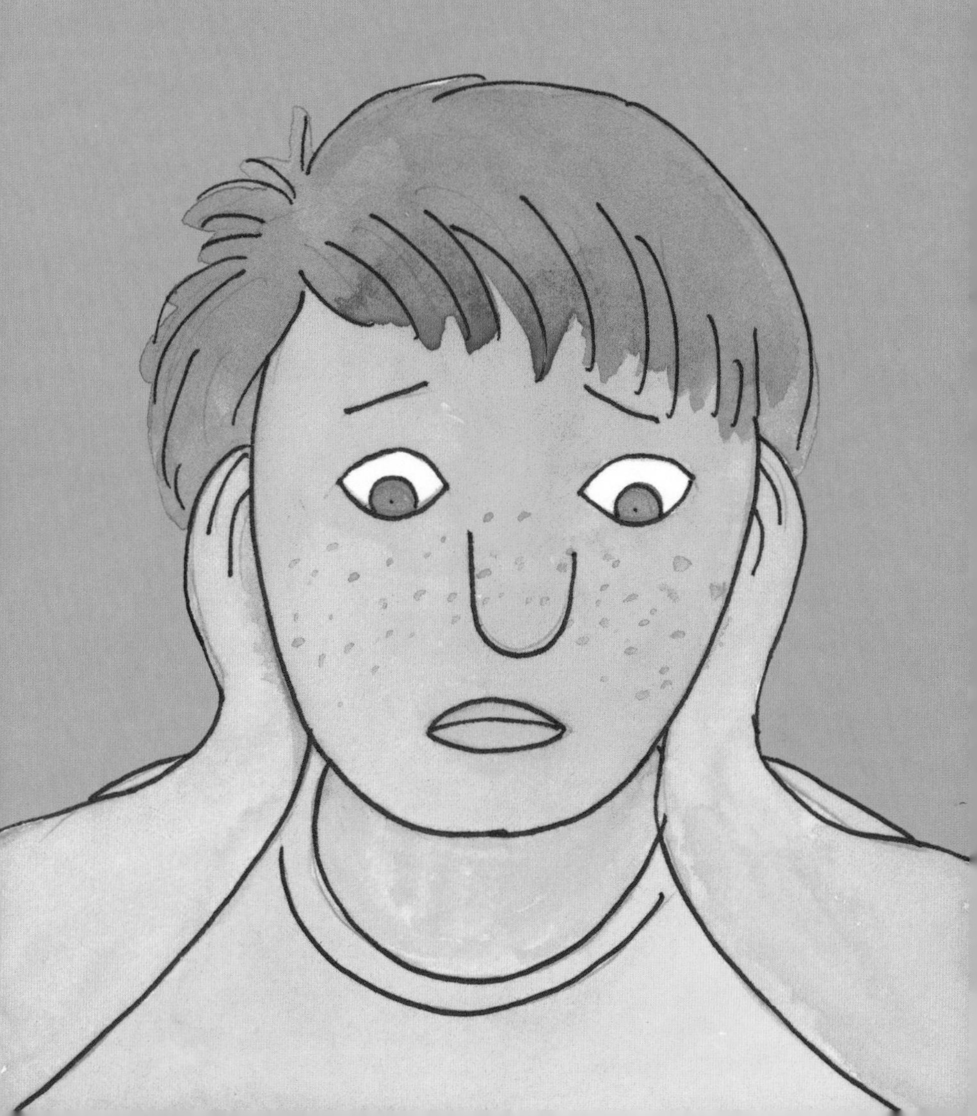

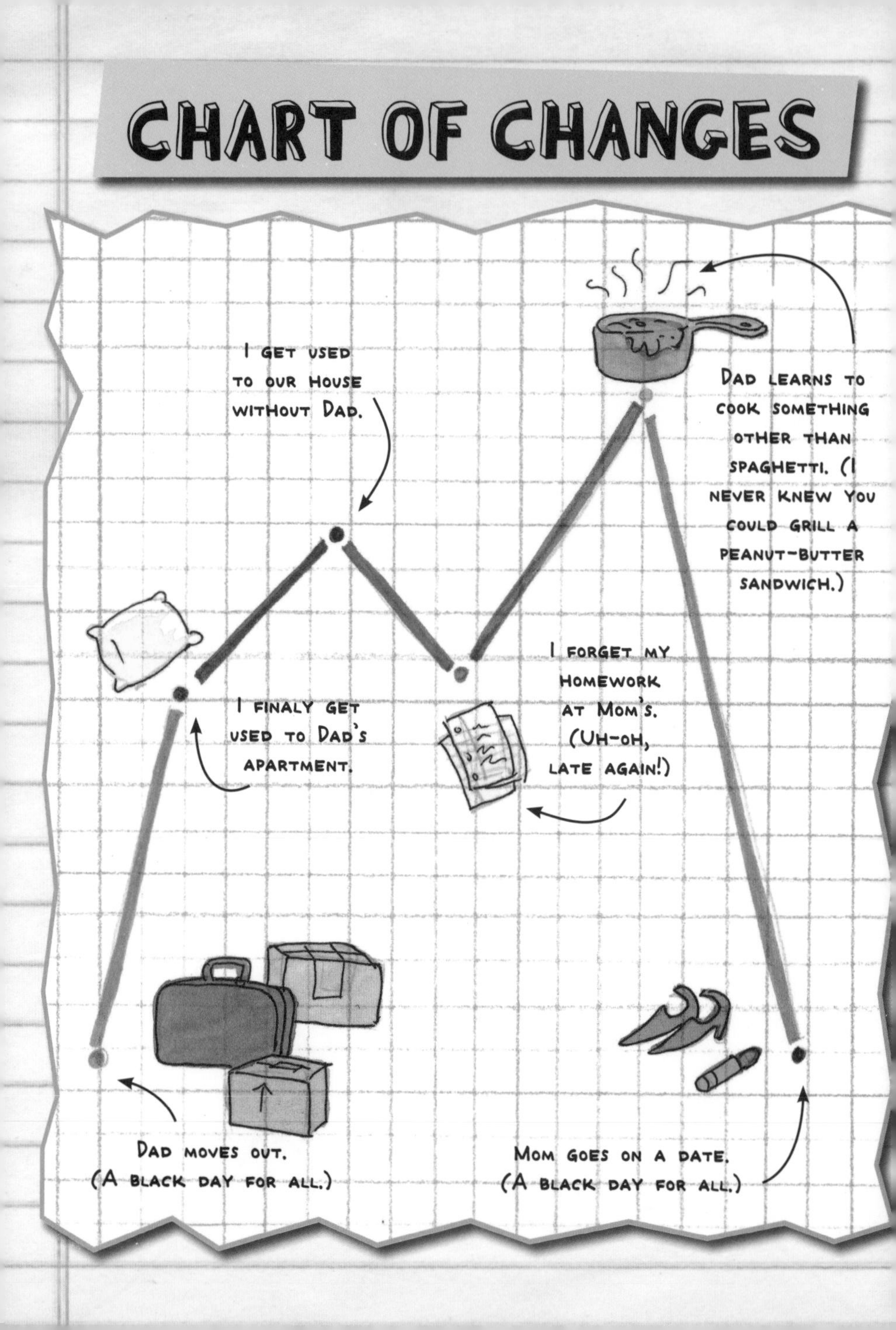
CHART OF CHANGES
I GET USED TO OUR HOUSE WITHOUT DAD.
DAD LEARNS TO COOK SOMETHING OTHER THAN SPAGHETTI. (I NEVER KNEW YOU COULD GRILL A PEANUT-BUTTER SANDWICH.)
I FORGET MY HOMEWORK AT MOM'S. (UH-OH, LATE AGAIN!)
I FINALY GET USED TO DAD'S APARTMENT.
DAD MOVES OUT. (A BLACK DAY FOR ALL.)
MOM GOES ON A DATE. (A BLACK DAY FOR ALL.)

But the very, very worst part of the weekend was coming back to Mom's house Sunday night. Usually Mom is practically waiting for Kevin and me at the door. This time she was rushing around and shoving stuff into the dishwasher as fast as she could. Stuff like two wine glasses and two plates. Stuff like she'd had somebody over for dinner. And I could smell that she was wearing perfume. Perfume!? She NEVER wears that junk. What I really smelled was a rat!

EXPLAIN THIS! DID YOU HAVE A DATE HERE? HAVE YOU BEEN SNEAKING AROUND BEHIND YOUR CHILDREN'S BACKS, LETTING STRANGE MEN COME INTO THIS HOUSE? YOU SHOULD BE ASHAMED OF YOURSELF!

EXHIBIT A: EMPTY WINE BOTTLE

She didn't look one bit ashamed or sorry.

In fact, she looked angry.

ARMS CROSSED (NEVER A GOOD SIGN)

IN A COLD VOICE:

MAX, YOU WILL NOT TALK TO ME THAT WAY!
I UNDERSTAND THAT THIS IS UPSETTING FOR YOU, BUT YOU HAVE NO RIGHT TO JUDGE ME. THIS IS MY HOME, TOO, AND I AM ENTITLED TO A LIFE.

That really steamed me! I stomped off to my room and slammed the door.

I stared at the ceiling for a long time.

If only I could control people and make them behave the way I want them to.

Heed my words, Earthling.
There is a way for you to succeed,
but much work remains to be done.
You must learn the power of mind
control. Fortunately for you, **I** am
an expert. Watch and learn!

I couldn't sleep, so I got up and started drawing the next episode of *Alien Eraser.* At least I can make HIM do whatever I want.

Alien Eraser
in
Monkey See,
Monkey Do
Alien Eraser is worshipped by the monkey men and acclaimed as their leader.
OOOH, OOOH! AAAH, AAAH!
Of course you do!
Translation: We will do as you command, O King.
Alien Eraser uses his formidable mental powers to communicate directly with the monkey minds . . .
You will find the power within you . . .
to be the best that you can be.
telepathically launching
OOH, OOH, AAH!
millions of years
OOH, OH! AH!
of gradual change
OH. AHA!
from monkey to man.
Look at me— I'm talking!
It's Alien Eraser's greatest accomplishment yet. But it's only the beginning.
Now I need clothes,
and a shave.
Man has the capacity to act with reason, but will he?
And what about Alien Eraser? Does he stay around to be revered? No! There is work to do on other planets.
I wish I had a cape!
I would look so much more dashing.
Alien Eraser is off to explore the far reaches of the galaxy. Find out what he discovers in the next issue of ALIEN ERASER!

That comic made me wonder, would I evolve differently if I lived only with Mom or only with Dad? Would I become a different person?

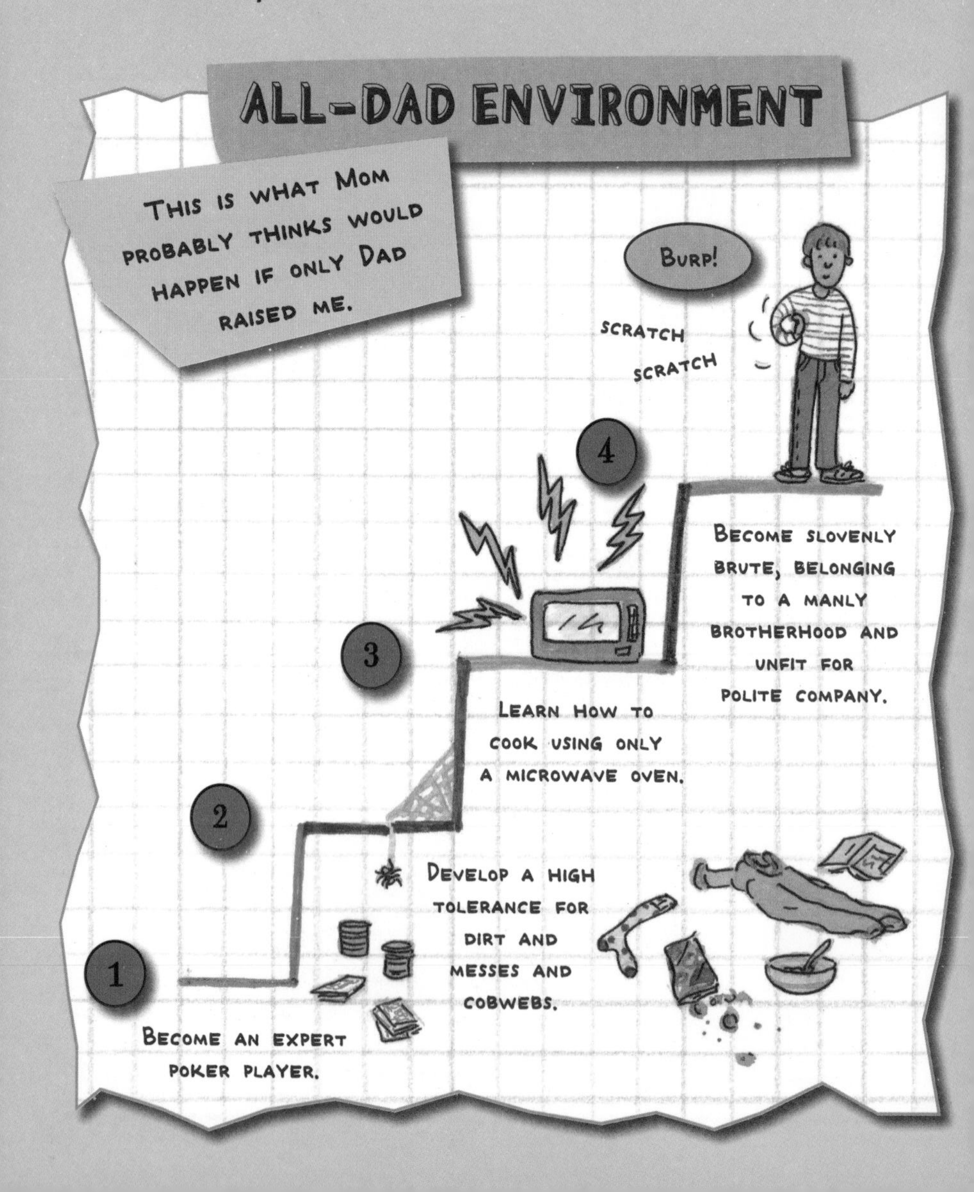

ALL-DAD ENVIRONMENT
THIS IS WHAT MOM PROBABLY THINKS WOULD HAPPEN IF ONLY DAD RAISED ME.
BURP!
SCRATCH
SCRATCH
4
BECOME SLOVENLY BRUTE, BELONGING TO A MANLY BROTHERHOOD AND UNFIT FOR POLITE COMPANY.
3
LEARN HOW TO COOK USING ONLY A MICROWAVE OVEN.
2
DEVELOP A HIGH TOLERANCE FOR DIRT AND MESSES AND COBWEBS.
1
BECOME AN EXPERT POKER PLAYER.

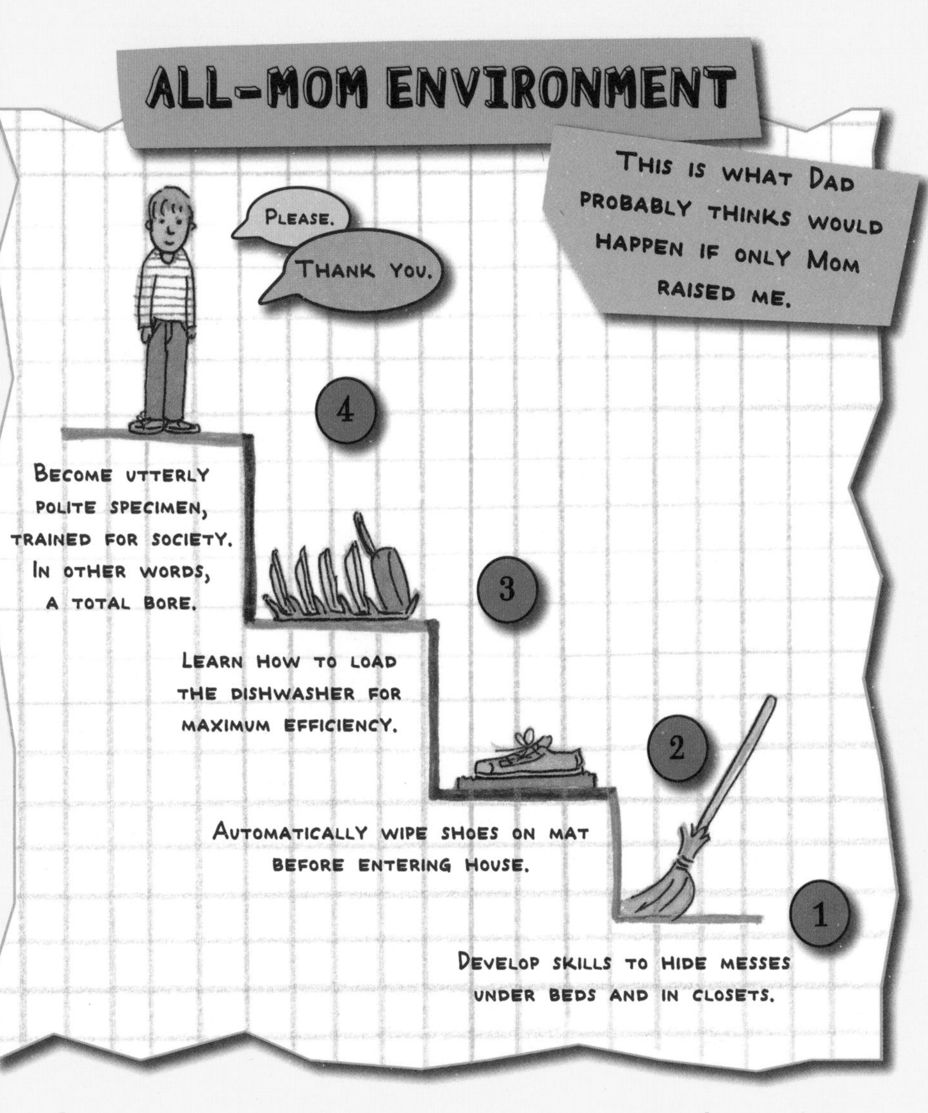

See, you can think of anything in terms of evolution!

If there's an evolution to a species and an evolution to a marriage, I guess there's probably an evolution to a divorce, and an evolution to a family.

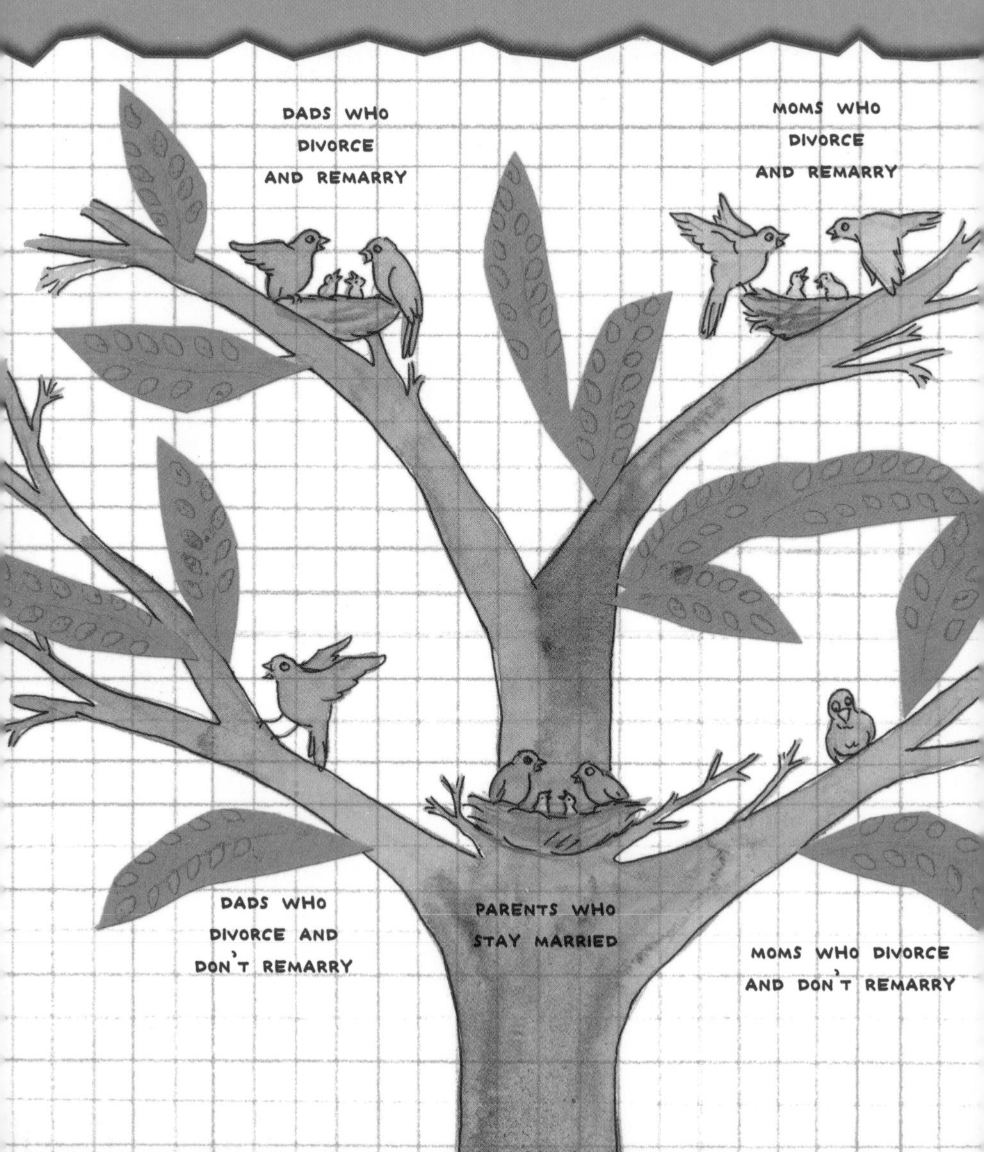

What will our family will look like in a year? Five years? Ten years?

My family is definitely changing, and I don't like it. Unfortunately for me, I'm not Alien Eraser, so I can't control people with my mind. I certainly can't control Mom or Dad. That's pretty obvious now. And who knows how **I'll** change. Look at Kevin—nice skin one day, pimply, crater-filled rubble-face the next. Well, that's a bad change. But changes can be good, too, I suppose.

TALLEST OF ALL

TALLER THAN DAD

TALLER THAN KEVIN

ABLE TO REACH TOP SHELF IN KITCHEN

ABLE TO RIDE FERRIS WHEEL

I AM GETTING TALLER.

Here's how I WANT to change:

1. Deeper voice—the deeper the better.

2. Muscle, muscle, and more muscle, so I can get as close to a Bionical Max as possible.

3. Taller—I want to be taller than Kevin, taller than Mom, taller even than Dad.

4. Become a great inventor, scientist, and comic-book artist—all of those things.

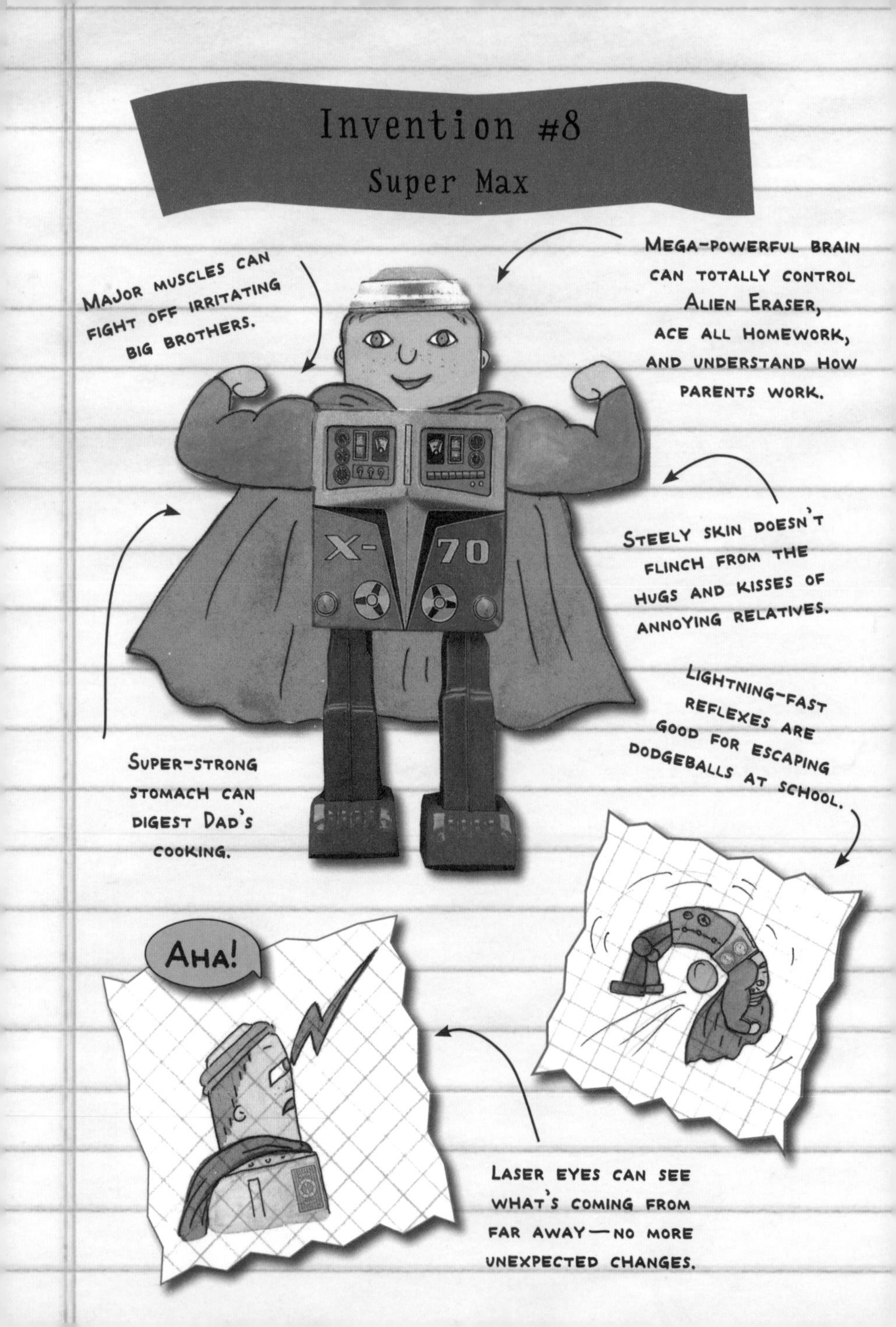
Invention #8
Super Max
Major muscles can fight off irritating big brothers.
Mega-powerful brain can totally control Alien Eraser, ace all homework, and understand how parents work.
X-70
Steely skin doesn't flinch from the hugs and kisses of annoying relatives.
Lightning-fast reflexes are good for escaping dodgeballs at school.
Super-strong stomach can digest Dad's cooking.
Aha!
Laser eyes can see what's coming from far away—no more unexpected changes.

I guess when you're in the middle of a change, you can't tell yet whether it's going to be a good one, a bad one, or a mixture of the two. You just have to try it, like an experiment, and see what happens.

And while I'm waiting to see how it all turns out, at least there's another kind of change I have total control over—THE EVOLUTION OF ALIEN ERASER!

HE STARTS OUT MILD-MANNERED AND POLITE . . .

BUT QUICKLY BECOMES IMPERIOUS (OMAR'S FANCY WORD FOR BOSSY) . . .

AND WITH TIME LEARNS TO USE HIS POWERS FOR THE GOOD OF ALL.

To Rob, who keeps me
constantly evolving

This is a work of fiction. Names, characters, places,
and incidents are either products of the author's imagination or,
if real, are used fictitiously.

First edition 2009

Library of Congress Cataloging-in-Publication Data is available.

Library of Congress Catalog Card Number 2008938433

ISBN 978-0-7636-3579-4 (hardcover)
ISBN 978-0-7636-4419-2 (paperback)

2 4 6 8 10 9 7 5 3 1

Printed in China

This book was typeset in Kosmic Plain One, with hand-lettered type by the author-illustrator.
The illustrations were done in colored pencil, gouache, watercolor, ink, and collage.

Candlewick Press
99 Dover Street
Somerville, Massachusetts 02144

visit us at www.candlewick.com

ALIEN ERASER
IN
NEW FRONTIERS
AFTER A WELL-DESERVED REST IN THE TROPICS . . .
ALIEN ERASER IS ONCE MORE READY FOR ACTION.
HMMM. WHAT CHALLENGE SHOULD I FACE NEXT? I'VE SURVIVED BEING CONFISCATED.
I'VE ESCAPED FROM MY ENEMY'S CLUTCHES.
IN THE MOST DARING EXPERIMENT OF ALL, I'VE HELPED HUMANITY EVOLVE FROM HAIRY APES, PLANTING THE SEEDS OF THE FUTURE.
AND I'VE EVOLVED INTO THE SUPERIOR BRAIN POWER THAT IS ALIEN ERASER.
WILL SUCH ACHIEVEMENTS BE ENOUGH FOR OUR HERO? WILL HE REST ON HIS LAURELS AND BECOME A GALACTIC TOURIST?

To find out where Alien Eraser ends up, what new dangers he faces, and how he evolves, look for the next issue of ALIEN ERASER!

Marissa Moss is the author-illustrator of the extremely popular Amelia's Notebook series, which now numbers twenty-eight titles. In addition, she has written and illustrated more than a dozen picture books, some historical fiction, and an ancient Egyptian mystery for older readers. The idea of writing stories in a notebook style came to her when she was buying school supplies for her son. She spotted a black-and-white composition book that reminded her of a notebook she had had when she was a kid. "So I bought it—for myself, not my son," she says, "and I wrote and drew what I remembered from when I was his age." She started drawing comics in high school, first in her notebook, then as a comic strip for the school paper, but the Max Disaster books have given her a chance to combine her love of inventions, experiments, and comics all in one place. Marissa Moss was born in Pennsylvania but moved to California when she was two and has lived there ever since. She studied art at San José State, history at the University of California at Berkeley, and art again at the California College of the Arts. Marissa Moss lives in the San Francisco Bay Area with her family.